A Houseful of Christmas

Unless Recalled Earlier

By Barbara Joosse
Illustrated by Betsy I

Henry Holt and Company • New

Every year the whole family
came to Granny's for Christmas.

For weeks, Granny baked . . .
and decorated . . .
and wrapped packages.
Edgar loved the Christmas fuss.

Fat Cat did not.
It was too noisy.

On Christmas morning,
Granny prepared her candied yam casserole
and set an extra leaf in the table.

Then she wound the grandfather clock,
sat down, and waited for her guests to arrive.
Edgar perched eagerly at the window,
while Fat Cat scowled under his favorite chair.

Tick tick tick
went the grandfather clock.
Flick flick flick
went the snowflakes,
hitting the window.

At last, they came—
Chatty Aunt Fanny
and her skinny sister, Clarisse.
Uncle Bert, the fireman,
and his brave fire dog, Walter.
Great-aunt Ruby, who smelled like
wild cherry cough drops.
Annie, Michael, and little Otto.
Aunt Ivy and her noisy boys—
Freddie, Dennie, and Kennie.
And Lambert, who had a soft, warm lap.

Everyone squeezed into the kitchen for Christmas dinner.
Uncle Bert carved his famous smoked turkey.
Clarisse tossed the salad greens,
and Granny passed her candied yam casserole.

Whhhhh went the wind.
Shhhhh went the snow.

After dinner, everyone opened presents.
There were lots of bows.

Granny played Christmas carols
on the accordion.
Everyone sang along,
except for Fat Cat, who sulked.

When it was time to leave,
Aunt Fanny opened the door.
The snow was mounded in front.
"There's too much snow to drive home," she said.

Granny looked at her big family and smiled.
"You can all sleep here!" she said.
"There's plenty of room on the floor."

Granny got out blankets and pillows,
and everyone settled down.

First came chatty Aunt Fanny,
who blabbed all the family secrets
to Great-aunt Ruby.
But Great-aunt Ruby had taken
out her hearing aid
and couldn't hear a word.

Tick tick tick went the grandfather clock.
Whhhhh went the wind.
Shhhhh went the snow.

Little Otto was afraid monsters
were crawling on Granny's floor.
He trembled under the covers.

Annie picked up Otto and held him close.
Michael rubbed his back.
No monsters could get Otto now!

Walter dreamed of his fire-dog days.
Riding the truck! Rescuing kittens!
As he dreamed, he jerked his legs
and thrashed around . . .
exactly like Uncle Bert.
Bert was dreaming of the glory days, too,
with Walter at his side.

Tick tick tick
went the grandfather clock.

Aunt Ivy couldn't sleep
with Freddie, Dennie, and Kennie
squirming beside her,

until Edgar scurried up to the boys,
gave them each a lick, and lay down.
He was long enough for everyone to reach.
The brothers patted Edgar
as they drifted off to sleep.

Tick tick tick went the grandfather clock.
Whhhhh went the wind.
Shhhhh went the snow.

Clarisse was thin as an icicle,
and cold as one, too.
She shivered under her blanket.
Lambert didn't need a blanket,
so he gave his to Clarisse.

Fat Cat spied Lambert's chest.
It was soft and warm.
He leaped up,
sprawled out,
and purred.

Tick tick tick
went the grandfather clock.
Shhhhh went the snow.

Granny listened to the clock
and the wind and the snow.
She listened to her family,
sleeping all around her.
She pulled the blanket up to her chin,
turned over
and over again.
"Edgar?" Granny called softly.

Edgar licked the sleeping boys one more time,
then scuttled up to Granny
and nestled in the crook of her arm.

Whhhhh went the wind,
but everyone was snug.

Shhhhh went the snow,
but everyone was together.

Tick tick tick
went the grandfather clock,
but everyone
was fast asleep.

Tick
    tick
        tick . . .

For Sylvia Beringer—
who sells kids joy,
who sells kids hope,
who sells kids books
—B. J.

In memory of my grandmothers,
Emma Dowler and Bertha "Nana" Reilly
—B. L.

Henry Holt and Company, LLC, *Publishers since 1866*
115 West 18th Street, New York, New York 10011
www.henryholt.com

Henry Holt is a registered trademark of Henry Holt and Company, LLC
Text copyright © 2001 by Barbara Joosse
Illustrations copyright © 2001 by Betsy Lewin
All rights reserved. Distributed in Canada by H. B. Fenn and Company Ltd.

Library of Congress Cataloging-in-Publication Data
Joosse, Barbara M.
A houseful of Christmas / Barbara Joosse; illustrated by Betsy Lewin.
Summary: Snowed in after sharing Christmas with Grandma
a houseful of relatives settles in for the night.
[1. Family—Fiction. 2. Grandmothers—Fiction. 3. Christmas—Fiction.
4. Sleep—Fiction. 5. Snow—Fiction.] I. Lewin, Betsy, ill. II. Title.
PZ7.J7435Ho   2001   [E]—dc21   00-47303

ISBN 0-8050-6391-9 / EAN 978-0-8050-6391-2 (hardcover)
3 5 7 9 10 8 6 4

ISBN 0-8050-7637-9 / EAN 978-0-8050-7637-0 (paperback)
1 3 5 7 9 10 8 6 4 2

First published in hardcover in 2001 by Henry Holt and Company
First paperback edition—2004
The artist used black line in pen and watercolor washes
on Strathmore paper to create the illustrations for this book.

Printed in the United States of America on acid-free paper. ∞